FALL LEAVES

To the loving memory of my parents, Mavis Young and Kerma C. Holland —L.H.

To Lily and Koen, who love adventure—and to Simon, who watches the leaves turn with me —E.M.

www.hmhco.com

The text of this book is set in Arta.
The illustrations are made with ink, yupo paper, light, and photography.

Library of Congress Cataloging-in-Publication Data
Holland, Loretta.
Fall leaves / by Loretta Holland ; illustrated by Elly MacKay.
pages cm
Summary: "Clever wordplay with homonyms puts autumn on display and captures
the art and science of season change."— Provided by publisher.
ISBN 978-0-544-10664-2
[1. Autumn—Fiction.] I. MacKay, Elly, illustrator. II. Title.
PZ7.H708665Fal 2014
[E]—dc23
2013036588

Manufactured in China
SCP 10 9 8 7 6 5 4 3 2 1
4500473799

FALL LEAVES

Loretta Holland   *illustrated by* Elly MacKay

HOUGHTON MIFFLIN HARCOURT
Boston   New York

When summer leaves . . .

FALL ARRIVES

In our universe, everything is always moving: the earth spins like a top while moving in a large circle around the sun. The sun also slowly moves in a circle around our galaxy. Our galaxy is slowly spinning too. All of these turnings make the sun's light come and go, getting closer and brighter to the earth at times or dimmer and farther away at other times. These changes create the cycles of days, nights, seasons, and years. In the Northern Hemisphere, the sun's light is moving south as *fall arrives* in late September.

BIRDS LEAVE

As the sun's light continues to move southward, days begin to get shorter and nights get longer. Some butterflies and birds leave to follow the sun, flying south for the winter.

LEAVES TWIST

Fall usually brings rain, which makes leaves twist and squirm on tree branches. The bottoms of the leaves look silver, like rain, and flash in the breeze as rain approaches.

RAIN FALLS

Fall rains come hard and steady, rushing off roofs like waterfalls. Sometimes it rains for days. When the *rain falls* for a long time, rivers and streams rise above their banks, and low-lying areas get covered with water. But most of the time it just puddles up in the road!

FLOWERS LEAVE

The blooms of most *flowers leave* in the fall. Many flowers such as tulips, daffodils, and others go to sleep for the winter, and when spring comes they begin to grow again. These types of flowers, called perennials, hibernate in the dirt when there is snow and ice on the ground. There are many animals that do not care much for winter either. They find a cozy spot and, like some flowers and trees, go to sleep until warm weather returns.

APPLES FALL

Fall is harvest time, when ripened *apples fall* from trees. Many fruits, grains, and vegetables are harvested so there will be plenty to eat over the winter. Sometimes the foods go straight from the garden to the table. Sometimes they are sold at roadside produce stands. And sometimes they go in big trucks or train cars to supermarkets all over the world.

LEAVES FALL

Deciduous trees such as maples, oaks, and hickories make their own food. Their leaves look very green because of a substance called chlorophyll. In these trees, water, carbon dioxide, and the chlorophyll from their leaves are mixed with sunlight to make a type of sugar. With that sugar the trees feed themselves. When fall comes and trees begin to prepare for winter, they eat less and the chlorophyll starts to drain from their leaves. This is when the true colors of the leaves come out, brightening up the woods until the *leaves fall* onto the ground.

FALL STAYS

Trees, plants, and animals are working hard to get ready for winter. But there is still time. Fall stays, regardless of the weather, until winter officially starts in late December.

LEAVES LEAVE

Most of the *leaves leave* by early November, blown down by the wind and rain. They carpet the woods and roads with brilliant color. Those that are still hanging on branches will fall when the trees stop feeding. The ends of the branches seal up, and the leaves snap right off.

Sun Leaves

By the time trees stand stark and shivery without their leafy covering, the sun has moved very far to the south. Even on clear days, the sun's rays are weak and give little warmth. Days are short now, and the sun *leaves* early each afternoon.

TEMPERATURE FALLS

Some days the sun shines pale yellow and some days it hides behind high clouds and there's a chill in the air. The *temperature falls* until one morning the ground and all the fallen leaves are white with frost.

SNOW FALLS

One day you may notice gray clouds hanging low in the sky. The smoke from chimneys will not rise up as it usually does but will drift down around the houses and hang in the tops of trees. That is because the air is so full of moisture that there's no room for smoke! Soon the sky will be dotted with snowflakes as the first *snow falls*.

FALL LEAVES

After three months of everything from sunny days to cool rains to snowfall, from green leaves to red and yellow leaves to bare branches, from flocks of birds flying overhead as they follow the sun, to birds looking for runaway seeds on the ground, *fall leaves*. It has been a special time of year, a busy season full of color and change.

ACTIVITY: Making Leaf Prints

If you would like to make leaf prints to hang in your room or on the refrigerator, or to make a pretty card to send to a friend,

go out in late summer while leaves are still fresh and green and pick a few from a tree you like, something that is well shaped and

solid without any tears. On a big piece of old newspaper, lay your leaf top-side down. You will be painting the bottom of the leaf.

Dip your brush (either an artist's brush or a foam brush will do) in paint and carefully color the bottom side of the leaf with a

thin layer. Lift the leaf carefully and place it paint-side down on your card or printing paper. Cover

it with a scrap of paper. With your fingers or with a roller (brayer), carefully press the

entire surface of the leaf onto your paper. Remove the scrap of paper and lift

the leaf carefully. Let your art dry. You will have a beautiful leaf print.

(Hint: If you use tempera or acrylic paint, cleanup is much easier.

Just use soap and water.)